Perdu

To Helen and Jane.
—R. J.

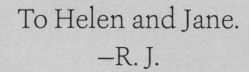

Published by
PEACHTREE PUBLISHING COMPANY INC.
1700 Chattahoochee Avenue
Atlanta, Georgia 30318-2112
www.peachtree-online.com

Text and illustrations © 2020 by Richard Jones

First Published in Great Britain in 2020 by Simon & Schuster UK Ltd
1st Floor, 222 Gray's Inn Road, London WC1X 8HB
A CBS Company

First United States version published in 2021 by Peachtree Publishing Company Inc.

The illustrations were rendered in paint and edited in
Adobe Photoshop.

Printed in January 2021 in China
10 9 8 7 6 5 4 3 2 1
First Edition

ISBN: 978-1-68263-248-2

Cataloging-in-Publication Data is available
from the Library of Congress.

Perdu

Richard Jones

PEACHTREE
ATLANTA

The sky was dark, the wind howled, and so did Perdu.

Poor Perdu. A little lost dog, all alone,
with no place to call home and nothing
to call his own but an old red scarf.

Rain fell on his night-black coat, and the grass was cold beneath his paws.

He watched a leaf tumble through the air

and land with a whispery tap on the water.

It danced in the current, spinning and turning as it floated away.

That leaf has a place to be, he thought.

But what about me?

Perdu decided to follow the leaf as it sailed on through the night—through fields and through woods, through grass short and tall.

The night faded away, black became blue,
and the sun began to rise.

The gentle stream that had been his friend
now rushed and raced away from him,
carrying his leaf out of sight.

The ground beneath his paws felt different now.

Tip, Tip, Tip, Tip, Tip, Tip, Tip, Tip

went his claws on the city concrete.

People rushed and raced around him.
The city is a busy place, the city is a noisy place,
the city is a big place when you are very small.

Everyone had somewhere to be.
I must find my place, thought Perdu.
I must find my somewhere.

All day he searched.

Inside. Outside.

Up

and

down.

But there was no place for Perdu.

"Get out!" they shouted.

"Go away!"

"Shoo!"

Poor Perdu. His little legs ached,
and his four paws were tired and sore.

His tummy rumbled and grumbled.
He *had* to find something to eat.

Perdu slipped inside.
Happy voices filled the warm air.
Tick, clack, clip went knives and forks.
The food smelled wonderful ...

Crash, bump, clang!

People growled and people barked.
"You silly dog. Look what you've done!"

Perdu felt the hard cold of the window
glass against his fur.

There was nowhere to go!

He cowered and trembled until ...

Scared, he growled back.

Scared, he snarled. So scared, he barked.

"Horrible animal!" the people shouted.

Run!

Dash!

Dodge!

Duck!

Poor Perdu, was there nowhere for him to belong?

When at last he stopped, he found he was in a park surrounded by tall shadowy trees.

He made himself a circle of pine cones, pebbles,
and leaves and curled up tight in the middle,
a scared little ball of worry.

A leaf fell gently on the grass beside him, and he looked up. There was a little girl and she was holding his scarf!

"Is this yours?" she asked softly.

Perdu looked into her kind eyes as she tied his scarf.

And all at once, he knew he was safe.

Together they turned to leave . . .

… and at last Perdu had a place to call home.